Barbara Ann Porte

"Leave That Cricket Be, Alan Lee"

PICTURES BY
Donna Ruff

GREENWILLOW BOOKS
New York

Airbrush, pastels, and colored pencils
were used for the full-color art.
The text type is Schneidler.

Printed in Singapore
by Tien Wah Press
First Edition
1 2 3 4 5 6 7 8 9 10

Library of Congress Cataloging-in-Publication Data
Porte, Barbara Ann.
"Leave that cricket be, Alan Lee" /
by Barbara Ann Porte ; pictures by Donna Ruff.
p. cm.
Summary: Alan Lee tries to catch the singing cricket
in his mother's office.
ISBN 0-688-11793-7 (trade).
ISBN 0-688-11794-5 (lib. bdg.)
[1. Crickets — Fiction.
2. Chinese Americans — Fiction.]
I. Ruff, Donna, ill.
II. Title.
PZ7.P7995Le   1993
[E] — dc20
92-29401   CIP   AC

THIS BOOK
IS FOR
MY AUNT BETTY
AND UNCLE HARRY,
WITH LOVE
—B. A. P.

FOR SARAH,
EMILY,
AND BRYAN
—D. R.

One night as Alan Lee got into bed, he heard a squeaky sound—*cree-cree-cree*. "Do you hear that?" he asked his mother.

"It's just a cricket singing. Now go to sleep, Alan Lee," his mother said. She tucked him in, kissed him good-night, and turned out the light.

Alan Lee went to sleep. By the time morning came, he'd forgotten all about the cricket. That night, though, as he was getting into bed, again he heard the cricket sing—*cree-cree-cree*.

"I'm going to find that cricket and watch it sing," Alan Lee told his parents the next day at breakfast.

"A cricket doesn't really sing," said his father. "It makes that squeaky sound by rubbing its wings together."

A cricket sings with its wings, thought Alan Lee. Now he wanted even more than before to find it.

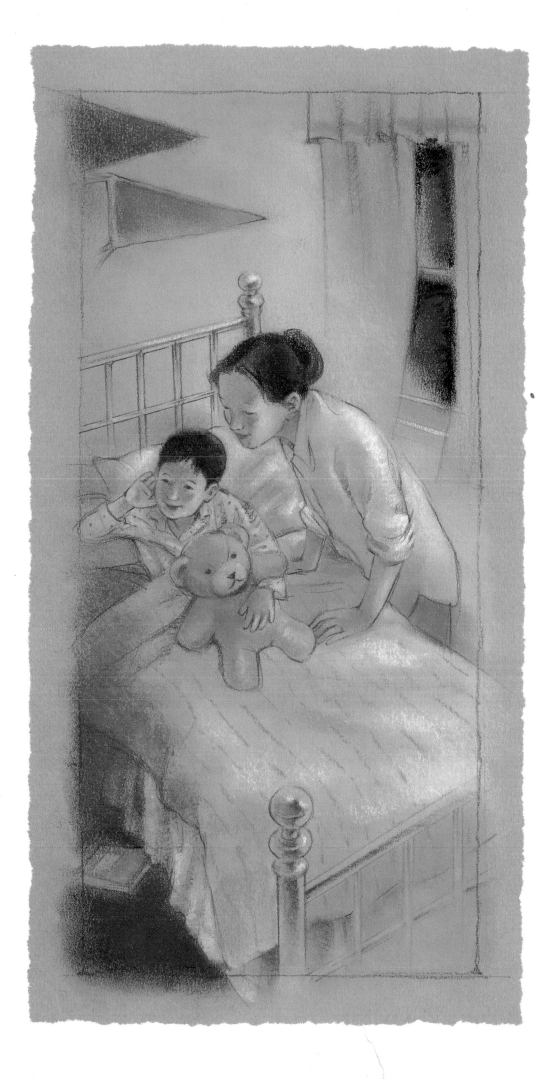

All morning he looked. He looked for it in his mother's office in the house, where she practiced law and kept her books. He looked for it in his father's basement studio, where he made porcelain pots and fired them. He looked in the kitchen and the living room, under carpets and behind furniture, inside cabinets. But all morning the cricket didn't sing, and Alan Lee couldn't find it.

In the afternoon Alan Lee did other things. He played with blocks, painted, rode his bicycle, and helped his father pull weeds in the garden. By nighttime Alan Lee was very tired. Just as he was getting into bed, he heard that cricket sing again—*cree-cree-cree*.

Alan Lee wanted to go find it, but his father said, "Leave that cricket be, Alan Lee. It's time for bed." Then he tucked him in, kissed him good-night, and turned out the light.

"Tomorrow, for sure, I'll find that cricket," Alan Lee said, speaking to himself. But the next day, as hard as he looked, he still couldn't find it. His father, though, found a picture of a cricket in a book to show him.

The day after that was Saturday.
Alan Lee's relatives came for dinner.
His great-uncle Clemson, who was
born in China, stayed overnight. As
Alan Lee helped him pull out the sofa
to make his bed, the cricket started
singing—*cree-cree-cree*.

"It's a lucky house that has crickets,"
Uncle Clem said. "That's what people
said in China when I was growing up."

"I think we have just one," said Alan Lee.

His uncle went on speaking. "When I
was your age, I made cricket cages."

"Cricket cages?" said Alan Lee.

"Oh, yes," said his uncle. "Barrowloads
of them. My father was a famous
cricket cage maker. I was his assistant.
We made cages from bamboo and
gourds, porcelain and ivory. We carved
cunning jade lids for some of them."

Then Alan Lee's uncle added, "Well, of course, after we came to this country, there was no call for cricket cages. We became jewelers instead. Jade bracelets and rings were our specialty. Sometimes we carved jade crickets and sold them for decoration."

"Yes, but why did people in China want cricket cages?" Alan Lee asked.

"To keep their crickets in, what else?" said his uncle. "People in China kept crickets for pets; sometimes for fighting, but mostly for singing. They were specially bred, born in cages, and very expensive. They dined on eggplant, cucumber slices, lettuce leaves, now and then a bit of chopped meat. There's nothing crickets won't eat, was what our customers told us."

Alan Lee was surprised to hear this. He'd asked his parents in the past if he could have a dog, or a cat, or even a goldfish. The idea of a cricket for a pet had not occurred to him. As he lay in bed that night, however, it was all he could think about.

The next day, after his uncle had gone home, Alan Lee told his parents his plan. "I'm going to catch that cricket for a pet. That way it will keep me company and can sing whenever it likes."

"It sings whenever it likes now," his mother pointed out. Even so, she emptied a large pickle jar and helped Alan Lee wash it out.

"It already keeps you company," his father said. Even so, he helped Alan Lee gather grass and sticks to line the jar, and together they pulled lettuce leaves and sliced a cucumber to put inside for food. Finally his father punched air holes in the jar lid so the cricket, once caught, could breathe.

Its house was ready now. All that was needed was the cricket.

Alan Lee spent the rest of the day trying to catch it. He carried the jar everywhere, looking. He looked underneath his mother's bookshelves and inside his father's pottery. He looked in closets, behind doors, and alongside the windowsills and baseboards. Now and then the cricket chirped—*cree-cree-cree*—but Alan Lee still couldn't find it. Every time he thought he knew exactly where the sound was coming from, it started coming from some other place.

Finally, after dinner, his mother said, "Leave that cricket be, Alan Lee. It's time for bed." She tucked him in, kissed him good-night, and turned out the light.

The cricket sang louder than ever— *cree-cree-cree*.

The next day, and the day after, and the day after that, Alan Lee kept looking. Five times he found the cricket. He was surprised to discover how high a cricket could jump, how fast it could move. No matter how fast Alan Lee moved, the cricket moved faster. Each time he thought he had it, it disappeared into a crack in the floor or behind a wall. Alan Lee was almost ready to give up.

Then Thursday morning, as he sat barefoot, his sneakers beside him, beneath his mother's desk, coloring in his new coloring book, out of the corner of one eye he thought he saw something jumping along the floor. It jumped from underneath the corner bookshelf, across the carpet, right into Alan Lee's empty sneaker. Before you could blink, Alan Lee had picked up his coloring book and placed it over the opening of his sneaker.

"I've got it," he shouted.

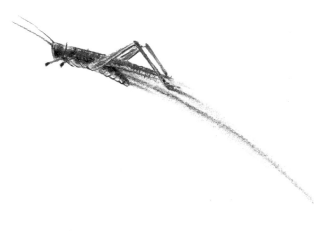

He was not really positive that what he had gotten was a cricket, but he believed that it was. He carefully carried his sneaker, the coloring book still on top, into the kitchen, where the open pickle jar was waiting. Very carefully he turned the sneaker upside down over the jar opening, then slid his coloring book out from beneath it. He jiggled the sneaker up and down and sideways, until finally something fell out. It fell down, down, down to the bottom of the jar and was lost among the sticks and grass. Alan Lee screwed on the jar lid and looked closely.

Now he could see he had indeed caught his cricket. It had righted itself and was scurrying around the jar on all six of its legs, feeling the glass with its two very long, very thin feelers, trying to feel its way out. Of course, there wasn't any way out, but the cricket didn't know that yet.

Alan Lee ran to show the cricket to his mother. She was in her bedroom, pinning up her hair.

"It's a good-looking cricket," she told him, peering at it closely.

"It isn't singing," Alan Lee said.

"Umm," said his mother. "Probably it just has to settle down." But she sounded doubtful as she said it.

Alan Lee took the cricket to the basement to show his father.

His father was throwing clay on his potter's wheel, but he stopped to look. "It's a very shiny cricket," he said.

"It isn't singing," said Alan Lee.

"Umm," said his father. "Probably it just has to get used to its jar." But he sounded doubtful as he said it.

For most of the rest of that day Alan Lee watched his cricket and waited for it to settle down, get used to its jar, and sing. By the time night came, though, that cricket still had not settled down, although now it ran more slowly, and it did not sing. When Alan Lee got into bed, he put the cricket jar on the floor beside him. He hoped his cricket would feel better in the morning.

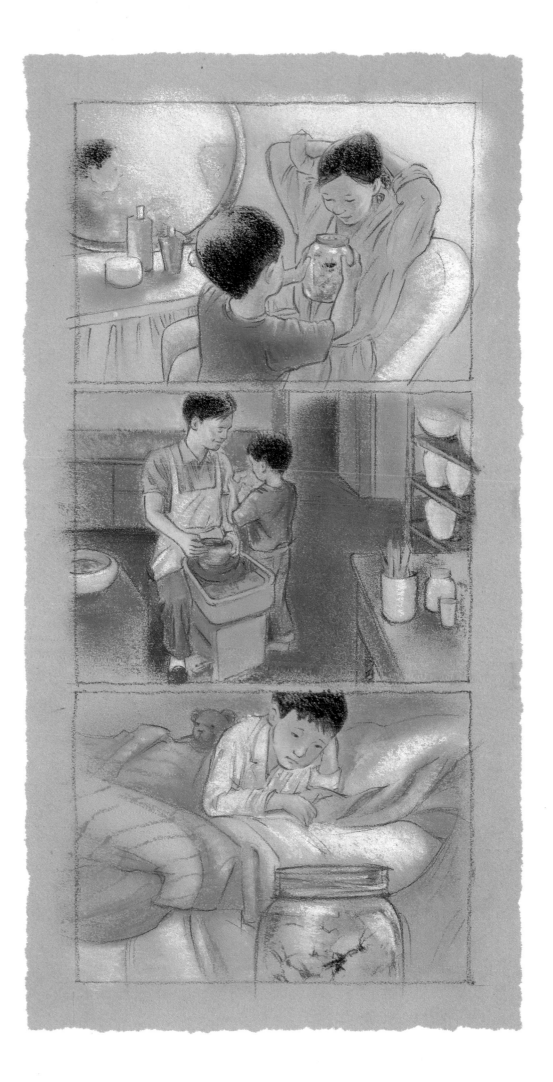

The next day when Alan Lee awoke, the first thing he did was look at his cricket jar.

Nothing was moving. The cricket was in the middle, absolutely still, partly hidden by a cucumber slice. Maybe it's dead, thought Alan Lee. He tapped the glass. The cricket jumped up right away and started scurrying in circles again, feeling with its feelers, trying to get out.

Alan Lee felt like crying. Instead, he got up, brushed his teeth, washed his face, and went downstairs for breakfast, carrying his cricket jar with him.

"How's that cricket doing?" asked his father.

"Has it settled down yet?" asked his mother.

Alan Lee only shook his head. He felt too sad to speak, also to eat. When he carried his cereal bowl from the table to the sink, most of his cereal was still in it.

Alan Lee went outdoors. He took his cricket with him. He set the jar down in some dirt. He thought his cricket might like being in the sun. He hoped it would sing, but it didn't. When lunchtime came, Alan Lee brought his cricket back indoors.

"Maybe if you eat something and rub your wings together, you'll feel better," he told it.

But the cricket didn't eat, and it didn't rub its wings together. By the time night came, it had given up running and looked sadder than ever.

Alan Lee looked sad himself. He lay in bed, listening to the quiet. After a while he fell asleep.

He awoke in the middle of the night. It was dark in the house and very still. Alan Lee got up, took the cricket in its jar, and tiptoed downstairs. He turned on the small lamp just inside his mother's office. He knelt beside her desk, unscrewed the lid, and laid the cricket jar on its side on the floor.

"Be free, cricket," Alan Lee said, sitting back on his heels.

Before he could blink, the cricket was out of the jar, taking large leaps, until it disappeared underneath the corner bookcase. It did not look back even once to say good-bye.

Alan Lee turned off the lamp and started back to his room. While he was still climbing the stairs, he heard a squeaky sound. At first it was so low he had to listen carefully to be sure. Then he knew for certain. *Cree-cree-cree*, came the noise. It was the cricket rubbing its wings together.

"Sing, cricket," Alan Lee whispered as he climbed into bed. Then, almost before you could blink, Alan Lee was sound asleep.

"How's that cricket today?" his father asked the next morning.

"Has it settled down yet?" asked his mother.

"It's fine, thank you. Yes," Alan Lee answered. "It wouldn't settle down in its jar, though, so I let it go."

Alan Lee tilted his head. "Listen!" he said. His parents did.

Cree-cree-cree, came that cricket sound, even though it was morning.

His mother stared at him. "Exactly where did you let that cricket go?" she asked.

"The same place I found it, in your office," Alan Lee told her.

"I see," said his mother. She was a bit surprised but didn't really mind. She liked the happy sounds that crickets make, and also, she believed they brought good luck.

Some weeks later Alan Lee's great-uncle Clemson came again to visit. After dinner Alan Lee's parents went to the movies.

"Did your cricket sing in its cage in China?" Alan Lee asked as his uncle tucked him into bed.

"My cricket?" said Uncle Clemson. "I never had a cricket. Did I ever say that I did? All I had were cricket cages, barrowloads of them. That's what I said. The customers who bought them had crickets. 'Crickets are too noisy, plus they cost too much,' my father told me anytime I asked for one. Once, when I was your age, I did try to catch a wild cricket, hoping to tame it. 'Leave that cricket be, Clemson,' my father told me. 'Pay attention to the cages.' Of course, he said it in Chinese. I paid attention. I always listened to my father."

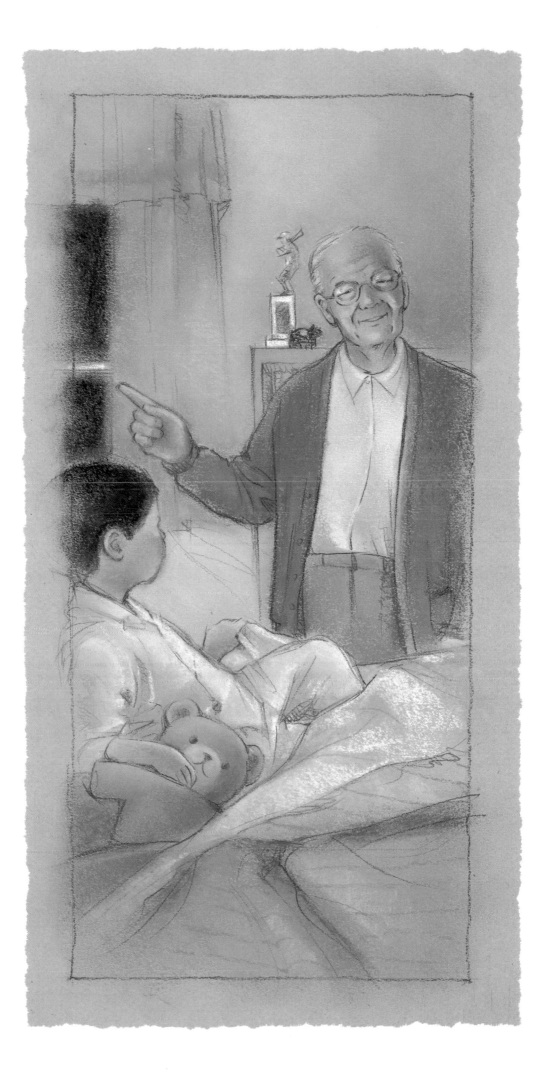

Uncle Clem tilted his head. "Listen," he said. Alan Lee did. *Cree-cree-cree*, came that cricket sound. Night had come.

"That's my cricket. I keep it in my mother's office. It's settled down now and sings whenever it likes," Alan Lee told his uncle.

"I'm glad to hear it," said Uncle Clem. "It's a lucky house that has crickets. That's what people said in China when I was growing up."

"Yes, I know," said Alan Lee, yawning. He was feeling rather lucky himself.

Uncle Clem kissed him good-night, turned out the light, and went downstairs to read the newspaper. It was very quiet in the house.

After a while the cricket resumed its singing. Probably it was feeling lucky, too. *Cree-cree-cree*, came the sound it made rubbing its wings together.

Only this time Alan Lee didn't hear it. He was sound asleep in his bed.